I Am Brave!

WRITTEN BY
Kelly Greenawalt

ART BY
Amariah Rauscher

✿ACORN™
SCHOLASTIC INC.

For my brave and adventurous sisters,
Shauna and Erin. — KG

To Jalen, who has always been brave. — AR

Text copyright © 2021 by Kelly Greenawalt
Illustrations copyright © 2021 by Amariah Rauscher

Library of Congress Cataloging-in-Publication Data
Names: Greenawalt, Kelly, author. | Rauscher, Amariah, illustrator. | Greenawalt, Kelly. Princess Truly; 5.
Title: I am brave! / by Kelly Greenawalt; illustrated by Amariah Rauscher.
Description: First edition. | New York: Acorn/Scholastic Inc., 2021. | Series: Princess Truly; 5 | Summary: In rhyming text super girl Princess Truly goes on a camping trip with little brother Ty and her dog, Sir Noodles; with her super powers she is not afraid of dark caves, bugs, or things that go bump in the night, which is a problem when she develops hiccups, and needs something to scare them away.
Identifiers: LCCN 2020049672 (print) | LCCN 2020049673 (ebook) | ISBN 9781338676891 (paperback) | ISBN 9781338676907 (library binding)
Subjects: LCSH: Princesses—Juvenile fiction. | African American girls—Juvenile fiction. | Camping—Juvenile fiction. | Courage—Juvenile fiction. | Superheroes—Juvenile fiction. | Hiccups—Juvenile fiction. | Brothers and sisters—Juvenile fiction. | Stories in rhyme. | CYAC: Stories in rhyme. | Princesses—Fiction. | African Americans—Fiction. | Camping—Fiction. | Courage—Fiction. | Superheroes—Fiction. | Brothers and sisters—Fiction. | Stories in rhyme. | LCGFT: Stories in rhyme.
Classification: LCC PZ8.3.G7495 Iah 2021 (print) | LCC PZ8.3.G7495 (ebook) | DDC [E]—dc23
LC record available at https://lccn.loc.gov/2020049672
LC ebook record available at https://lccn.loc.gov/2020049673

10 9 8 7 6 5 4 3 2   21 22 23 24 25

Printed in China   62

First edition, November 2021

Edited by Rachel Matson
Book design by Sarah Dvojack

Let's Go Camping!

I am Princess Truly.
I am brave, smart, and strong.

We are going camping.

Ty wants to come along.

Off to the woods we go!
We have a lot to take.

We walk down the long trail
and set up by the lake.

First, we put up the tent.

Then it's time to unpack.

Next we build a fire,

and make a yummy snack.

Let's go out and explore.
Sir Noodles finds a cave.

I want to go inside,
but Ty does not feel brave.

Ty does not like the dark.
He wants to leave right now.

Ty will not go inside.
No way! No thanks! No how!

I have a great idea.
My curls begin to glow.

I hold his hand real tight.
Into the cave we go!

We find a hidden lake.
We climb the waterfall.

Ty does not feel afraid.
He is brave after all!

Hiccup!

hiccup

I have the hiccups bad.
I want to make them go.

I fill my cheeks with air.
I let it out real slow.

hiccup

Ty has a great idea.
He will scare them away.

But I am just too brave.
I think they're here to stay.

Lizards do not scare me.

I think big bugs are neat.

I'm not afraid of snakes.

I think spiders are sweet.

Sir Noodles will help Ty.
They hide behind a tree.

When I walk in the woods,
they jump out to scare me.

23

hiccup

You two cannot trick me.
I am too brave to scare.

But what is up the hill?
Look out! There is a bear!

I jump and then I yell!
My hiccups go away.

Brave girls can get scared, too.
That bear cub saved the day!

A Spooky Story

It's time to go to bed.
The stars and moon shine bright.

We tell spooky stories,
and then we say good night.

We climb into our tent.

I toss and turn around.

Then I see a shadow
and hear a creepy sound.

Ty whispers, "What is that?"
Sir Noodles starts to shake.

It looks big and scary.
It's over by the lake.

I am a brave princess.
My magic curls shine bright.

I climb out of the tent
and head into the night.

Is it a lake monster?
The shadow is growing.

I shine my red flashlight.
I see two eyes glowing!

It is not a monster!
It is just a big frog.

He sticks out his long tongue.
He jumps off of his log.

I hear a scary noise.
I shine my light to see.

Something strange is moving.
It tries to follow me!

Is it a lake monster?

Is it another frog?

I giggle when I see,
it's just my dirty dog.

About the Creators

Kelly Greenawalt is the mother of seven amazing kids. She lives in Texas with her family. Princess Truly was inspired by her brave daughters, who are always up for adventure.

Amariah Rauscher is brave most of the time. She isn't afraid of spiders or snakes, and is only a tiny bit afraid of heights. Amariah is the mom of two girls. She spends most of her time drawing, painting, and reading books.

Read these picture books featuring Princess Truly!

YOU CAN DRAW A BEAR!

1 Draw two lines for the eyes, and a triangle for the nose.

2 Add the mouth.

3 Draw two half circles for the ears. Add two smaller circles inside.

4 Connect the two ears with a line.

5 Finish drawing the outline of the face.

6 Color in your drawing!

WHAT'S YOUR STORY?

Princess Truly can't get rid of her hiccups. Imagine that **you** have the hiccups! How would you get rid of them? Would a friend be able to scare you? Write and draw your story!